D1015871

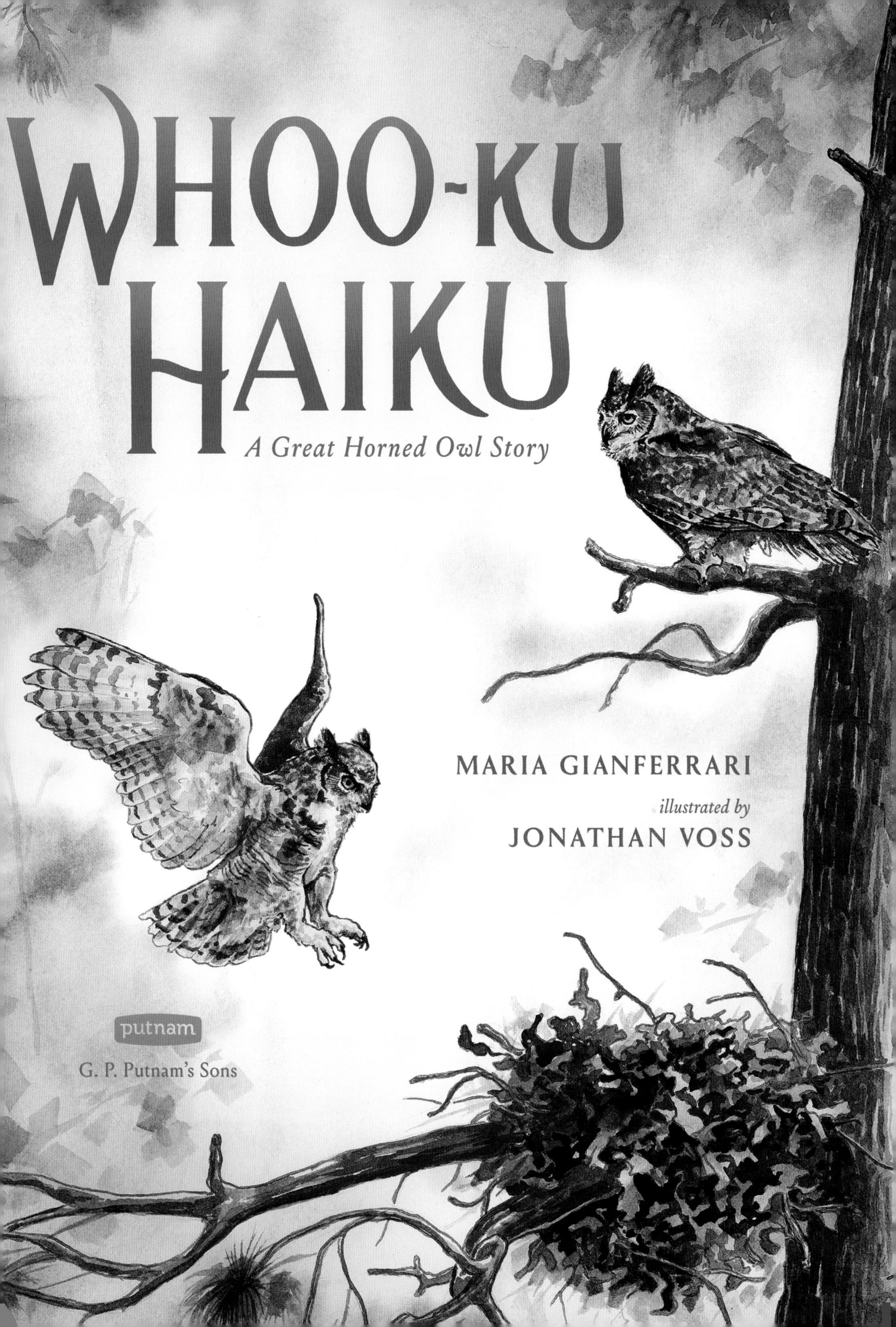

WHOO-KU HAIKU

A Great Horned Owl Story

MARIA GIANFERRARI

illustrated by

JONATHAN VOSS

putnam

G. P. Putnam's Sons

A great horned owl pair
Finds squirrel's nest of oak leaves
Perched high in a pine.

Papa adds birch bark
Nest blanketed with feathers
Snow sleeps on the ground.

Crows dive-bomb and caw
Mama dodges, ducks her head
This is now her home.

Mama calls her mate
Papa delivers a snake
Belly full, she preens.

Mama lays an egg
In the starlight it glistens
A moon of its own.

Today there are three
Papa hunts while Mama broods
Wind whips; eggs are warm.

Crows attack again
Mama mantles; egg falls out
Raccoon finds dinner.

Mama shrieks a song
And rolls the eggs together
Two eggs feels empty.

Pip. Pip. Pip. Poking.
A hole, cracking. Cracking. Crack!
Pink owlet pecks out.

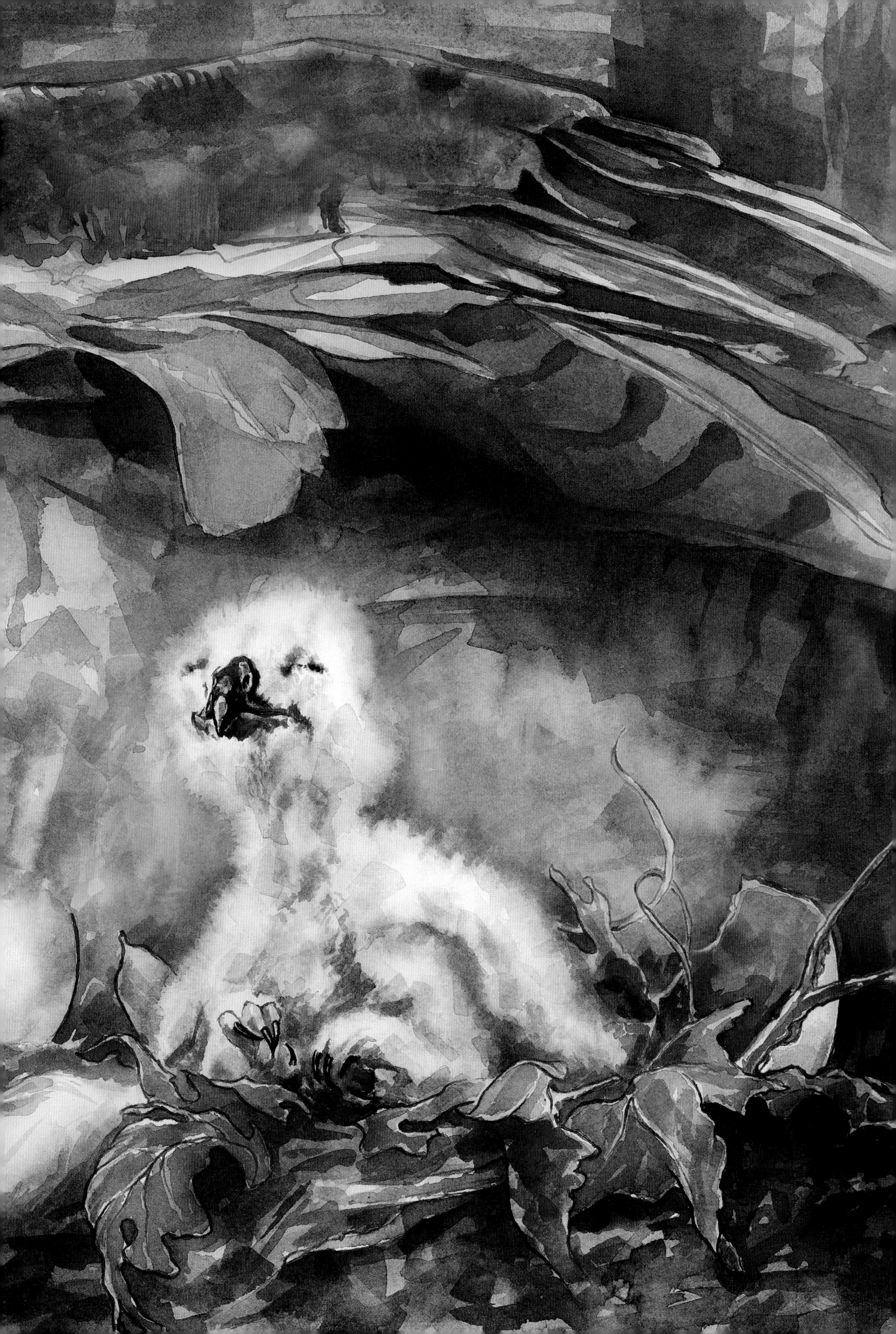

Now two owlets rest
Dandelion tufts of down
Mama's chest is best.

Mama beaks the prey
Owlets grab, tug and tussle
One owlet hungers.

In the rain they wait
Beneath umbrella of wings
Safe and warm and snug.

Mama plucks at plumes
Papa alights on the nest
A skunk for supper.

Hawk circling above
Swaying heads from side to side
Owlets all alone.

Owlets raise their wings
Shadow covers; hawk hovers
Screech! Hiss! Hawk is gone.

Trying out her wings
Beating, leaping, teetering
Owlet bobs and springs.

Slipping to the ground
Eeping, flapping, fluttering
Nest far, far away.

Red fox is watching
Red fox is sneaking-slinking
Red fox is crouching . . .

Red fox launches—pounce!
Up! Down! Up! Down! Up! Down! Up!
Mama screams and dives.

Talons nick; fox flees
Owlet jumps and pumps her wings
At last she is home!

Moonlit yellow eyes
Owl family huddles-cuddles
In their cozy nest.

Together is best
Clan complete; twilight retreats
Full moon is blooming.

Sprouted ear tufts twitch
Pinecones whispering autumn
Soon fledgling owls fly.

Into the night sky
To find a home of their own
Whoo-whoo-whoo-WHOOO-ku.

Want to know more about great horned owls?

HOME SWEET HOME The most common owl in North America, the great horned owl lives as far north as Canada and parts of Alaska, and south into Mexico, Central and South America.

WHOSE NEST IS BEST? Great horned owls don't make their own nests—they use the abandoned nests of squirrels or birds. They choose nesting sites in wooded areas bordering fields, meadows, or other open areas for better hunting. Nesting begins in January or February.

BORN TO HUNT Great horned owls are fierce predators with bodies made for hunting: strong feet with locking tendons, razor-sharp claws called talons for gripping prey, and bladed beaks like knives for tearing flesh. When great horned owls catch prey, they mantle, or hold out their wings like a cloak, to protect their prey. They also mantle when they feel threatened, to make themselves look bigger.

ENORMOUS EYES Although it's smaller than a toddler, a great horned owl has eyes as big as an adult human's. If you had eyes like a great horned owl's, they'd be as big as grapefruits! Large eyes and pupils help them hunt in low-light conditions.

HEIGHTENED HEARING Though great horned owls are unable to see in total darkness, they have keen hearing to detect prey. The flat disc feathers on their rounded faces act like satellite dishes, directing sounds to their ears on the sides of their heads. They don't actually have horns—those are their ear tufts.

LIGHT AS A FEATHER Great horned owls' feathers have many handy features. Special fringe feathers on their wings separate like a comb to let air pass through so they can fly silently and surprise their prey. Soft feathers insulate them against the cold. Barred belly markings resemble the pattern of tree bark, serving as camouflage.

ROOSTING = RESTING Great horned owls roost, or rest, in trees, snags (fallen trees), or stumps. While roosting, they are often mobbed by birds such as crows, ravens, blue jays, and other songbirds.

LAY AN EGG Great horned owls usually lay a clutch of one to four eggs. A female lays an egg every two days. The older eggs hatch first; the larger the chick, the better able it is to compete for its parents' food. Females incubate the eggs to keep them warm for about one month. All birds have an egg tooth, a small lump on their beaks to help poke through the eggshell, that falls off shortly after hatching.

LOOK WHO'S HERE! Owlets are born blind, but open their eyes when they're around ten days old. Thicker downy feathers develop after one to two weeks. At six weeks, owlets "branch," or venture onto branches outside the nest, though they will not be able to fly for another ten to twelve weeks.

WHO'S HUNGRY? Great horned owls have the most varied diet of all raptors (birds of prey). In the suburbs, great horned owls may eat rabbits, raccoons, skunks, woodchucks, geese, owls, other birds, or bats. Beware—they even eat house cats and small dogs! In a city, they favor skunks, rats, mice, and pigeons. Desert-dwelling great horned owls dine on scorpions, hares, lizards, and snakes. In the tundra, snowshoe hares, grouse, and ptarmigan are the main courses. Because of their diverse diet, they are highly adaptable and can live in a variety of habitats: woodlands, wetlands, deserts, grasslands, clearings, and fields.

NO NEED TO CHEW! Owls can't chew their food. They swallow smaller prey whole, while larger prey is torn before swallowing. They spit up what they can't digest—fur, bones, teeth, and feathers—in pellets. Ornithologists (bird scientists) understand owls' eating habits by analyzing their pellets.

WHAT A HOOT! The great horned owl's best-known call is "hoo-hoo-HOOOOO-hoo," a territorial call. They also hiss, scream, whistle, bark, chuckle, coo, and squawk. They may growl, make guttural noises, or clap and snap their bills to scare off humans and predators.

BOOKS

Pringle, Laurence. *Owls! Strange and Wonderful.* Honesdale, Pa.: Boyds Mills Press, 2016.
Rashid, Scott. *The Great Horned Owl: An In-Depth Study.* Atglen, Pa.: Schiffer Publishing, Ltd., 2015.
Smith, Dwight G. *Wild Bird Guides: Great Horned Owl.* Mechanicsburg, Pa.: Stackpole Books, 2002.
Weidensaul, Scott. *Peterson Reference Guide to Owls of North America and the Caribbean.* Boston: Houghton Mifflin Harcourt, 2015.

WEBSITES

The Cornell Lab of Ornithology's All About Birds: www.allaboutbirds.org/guide/Great_Horned_Owl/
The Owl Pages: www.owlpages.com/owls/species.php?s=1220
National Geographic: www.nationalgeographic.com/animals/birds/g/great-horned-owl/

VIDEOS

Want to watch great horned owls raise their owlets? Check out the Cornell Lab of Ornithology's Savannah Owl Cam highlights here:
https://www.youtube.com/playlist?list=PLgSpqOFj1Ta6hyH1uumDAJYW74-_qqIaR
And here: http://cams.allaboutbirds.org/channel/46/Great_Horned_Owls/

WHOO's the best critique group? CP, Crumpled Paper critique, that's who! Many thanks to my trusted friends and critique partners: Lisa Robinson, Andrea Wang, Lois Sepahban, Abigail Calkins Aguirre and Sheri Dillard. And special thanks and love always to Anya, who came up with the title! —M.G.

In memory of my grandfather Herbert Everett Abbott, who was always as tender as he was strong. —J.V.

G. P. Putnam's Sons
An imprint of Penguin Random House LLC, New York

Visit us online at penguinrandomhouse.com

Library of Congress Cataloging-in-Publication Data
Names: Gianferrari, Maria, author. | Voss, Jonathan D., illustrator. | Title: Whoo-ku haiku : a great horned owl story / Maria Gianferrari ; illustrated by Jonathan Voss. | Other titles: Whoo ku haiku | Description: New York, NY : G. P. Putnam's Sons, [2020] | Audience: Ages 5–8. | Audience: K to grade 3. | Includes bibliographical references. | Identifiers: LCCN 2017061070 | ISBN 9780399548420 (hardcover) | ISBN 9780399548437 | ISBN 9780399548451
Subjects: LCSH: Great horned owl—Juvenile literature. | Great horned owl—Juvenile poetry. | Haiku. | Children's poetry. | CYAC: Owls.
Classification: LCC QL696.S83 G53 2019 | DDC 598.9/7—dc23
LC record available at https://lccn.loc.gov/2017061070

Manufactured in China by RR Donnelley Asia Printing Solutions Ltd.
ISBN 9780399548420
1 3 5 7 9 10 8 6 4 2

The illustrations were created using sepia ink and watercolor on Arches 300# hot press watercolor paper. Color was added digitally.
Text set in Louize. Design by Semadar Megged and Eileen Savage.